The Magic TUNNEL

By CAROLINE D. EMERSON

Illustrated by JERRY ROBINSON

SCHOLASTIC BOOK SERVICES

NEW YORK · TORONTO · LONDON · AUCKLAND · SYDNEY · TOKYO

ISBN: 0-590-01351-3

13 12 11 10   9/7 0 1 2/8

Printed in U.S.A.   21

CONTENTS

By the same author:

FATHER'S BIG IMPROVEMENTS

Available through Scholastic Book Services, Inc.

*O*n an August day in 1664, the English turned their guns on the little Dutch village of New Amsterdam and demanded its surrender. Enraged but helpless, Governor Peter Stuyvesant had to yield. New Amsterdam became New York.

In the three hundred years from then to now, a small bustling village has become one of the great cities of the world. In the same fine harbor where small ships rode in with wind-filled sails, great ocean liners now come and go.

Three hundred years!

What was it like to live in old New Amsterdam so long ago?

Go through the magic tunnel now — and see!

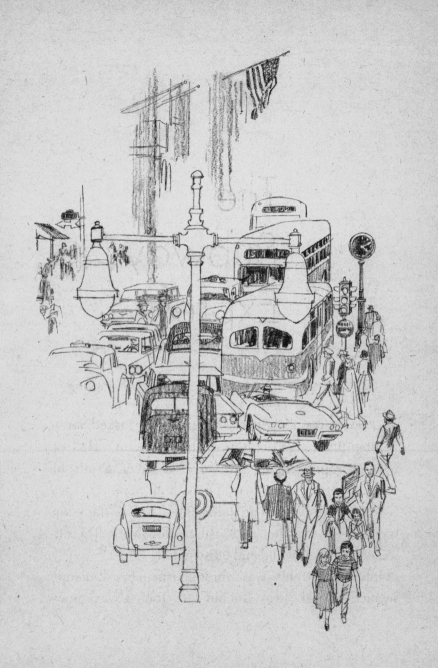

The
Subway
Express

"Do you really think we ought to go?" asked Sarah.

John paid no attention to the question. He was walking rapidly along the crowded street. Sarah, his cousin, trotted along just behind him. Sarah was ten, two years younger than John. She lived in the country, and this was her first visit to New York. The city seemed very crowded and noisy to her.

John picked his way through the crowd. People seemed to make way for him, for John always knew exactly where he wanted to go and what he wanted to do. It was different with Sarah. She was small, and people kept bumping into her by mistake. "I'd say there were too many people in New York," thought Sarah. "Much too many."

John stopped for the lights to change. Sarah looked questioningly up at him. Again she asked, "Do you really think we ought to go? What will our mothers say?"

Lights flashed from red to green. John gripped Sarah by the arm and hurried her past the hot noses of the waiting cars. Even cars seemed more impatient in the city than in the country!

When they reached the curb in safety, John said firmly, "Come over here by the subway entrance, where people won't be bumping into you, and let's talk this over."

John stopped by a long flight of stairs that led down into the earth. Sarah peered into the dismal-looking hole.

"Is that the subway?" she asked.

"Yes," said John, "and this train goes down to Battery Park, where we can see the harbor and the Statue of Liberty. Come on!"

"But — but — " began Sarah again.

"Now see here," said John, "when our mothers went off shopping, they said that I could take you downtown and show you Battery Park and the Statue of Liberty, didn't they? Mother gave me the money and told me just what to do, didn't she?"

"Y-es," admitted Sarah, "only she thought Aunt Mary would go with us."

"Well, Aunt Mary got called home because her little girl was so sick, didn't she?" demanded John. "Mother never said we couldn't go alone, did she?"

"No-o — " said Sarah slowly.

"I've been on the subway alone lots of times," John said. "Don't you want to see Battery Park and the Statue of Liberty and Brooklyn Bridge and everything?"

"Y-y-yes," said Sarah.

"Well, come on then," said John. "Don't worry. I'll take care of you, and I'll tell you all about the part of town we're going to. It's the old part of New York, you know."

John warmed to his subject. He was determined to quiet Sarah's questionings. John did not like to have his plans fail.

"It was down there by Battery Park where the first white people who came here built their town. They were Dutch, you know, and they called the town New Amsterdam," John told her.

"Then how did the city get to be New York?" asked Sarah, but John was growing impatient.

A crowd of people came up the subway stairs.

"Oh, come on!" cried John. "We've missed one train already."

John plunged down the stairs. Sarah hesitated for a moment and then followed him. When she reached the bottom of the stairs, John was fast disappearing down a long passageway, like the rabbit in *Alice in Wonderland*. Sarah ran after him. She caught up with him at the turnstile. John put a subway token in the coin box for her and pushed her through ahead of him. Then he led her down the length of the long, dim platform.

"I always like to ride in the front car," he explained.

In another minute, bright lights appeared way down the track. The lights were coming rapidly toward them, and in a few moments a train came rushing into the station. Sarah braced herself as the cars roared past her like a hurricane. Then the train stopped, and doors opened mysteriously in its side.

"It's an express train! Just what we want!" cried John.

He steered Sarah into one of the cars. The door closed behind them, and the train started with a jerk. The train was already crowded. Sarah found herself standing among many people. Most of them held onto straps, to keep from falling as the train swayed this way and that.

John and Sarah began to walk from car to car. John led Sarah skillfully between people until the two of them reached the very first car. John stationed himself at the front window and Sarah stood beside him. As she looked out, she gave a little gasp of amazement.

She could see far, far down the track, down the mysterious tunnel through which they sped. Crowds

and people were forgotten as she watched the lights of the long passageway ahead. The two lines of tracks gleamed like silver from the reflected lights. The train seemed to be chasing the darkness and never catching up with it.

"Think of it," Sarah said to herself, for it was far too noisy to say anything to John, "we're racing through the earth like magic, and up above us are streets and high buildings and trucks and buses and all of New York!"

And so John and Sarah started off on their subway trip. Little did they know where they were to go that day, or what strange sights they were to see!

"Where Are We?"

THE TRAIN BEGAN TO RUN more slowly. The noise grew less. Then the train slipped into an Aladdin's cave of a station, all bright with lights. The train came slowly to a stop. There was a hurry of people getting off and on. Sarah turned curiously to watch them. Where were they going, where did they live, and what were they doing anyway? They seemed more like shadows than real people to her. The doors of the cars began to slide shut. One or two people came running across the platform at the last minute and squeezed in just before the door closed. Then the train was off again, tearing through the earth.

Other trains flashed past. Trains going in the other direction whizzed by with a roar. On and on they all went.

"What a mad family of trains," Sarah thought, "and all living underground!"

When the train was in motion, there was far too much noise to hear anything that was said, but as it slowed down at the next station John turned toward Sarah. His eyes were very bright, and his hair seemed to stand even more on end than usual.

"You know," he began in a sudden burst of confidence, "when I stand up in the front of the car this way, I imagine I'm running the train. I'm the one who makes the thing go!"

"Oh —" murmured Sarah in surprise at the idea. She did not feel at all as though she would like to run the train.

John went on. "And you know," he said, "I imagine that I can run the train anywhere I want to go. I could run it right through to Florida, to the North Pole, or under the Atlantic Ocean, like a submarine."

Sarah listened, wide-eyed. It made her feel a little uneasy.

"You know, Sarah," John went on, "there's supposed to be a spot somewhere in this first car — they say that if you could find it and make a wish, standing right on that special spot, the train would go anywhere you wanted it to go!"

There was no more time for talk, for the train was starting and the noise began again. John turned back to the window and fixed his eyes on the lights and the gleaming rails. He watched the track ahead as though a spell held him. On and on they went.

For a minute Sarah thought about what John had said. "Well," she murmured softly to herself, "if I had a wish, I'd wish I could go somewhere in this city where it wasn't so crowded, and where there weren't so many people!"

All of a sudden the train seemed to start running faster and faster. Then it gave a jerk that nearly threw Sarah off her feet. She grabbed John's arm to keep from falling.

"What's happening?" she cried, but her voice was lost in the noise.

Slowly the children realized what *was* happening. The train was running in the opposite direction from

the one in which they had been going! They were moving backwards rapidly. Instead of being at the front end, they were standing at the very rear of the last car.

"That's funny!" John muttered.

Sarah looked about her in surprise. What she saw made her open her eyes wide in amazement. The car in which they stood was empty!

She put her mouth close to John's ear and shouted, "John, look! We're the only people left!"

The train rushed on. Station after station went flashing past. Then the train made a swing round a curve in the track. Looking back at the cars behind them, the children could see almost the entire train. Every car behind them was empty!

"Wait here," John shouted to Sarah. He began to make his way from car to car, down the long length of the train. In each car he peered into the little compartment where a motorman or a guard might be. All the compartments were empty! Down the track through the depths of the earth they were speeding, with no one in control.

"Whew!" John whistled. Then he turned and made his way slowly back, through car after car, to Sarah.

Sarah put her lips close to John's ear again and called, "Where do you suppose we are by now?"

John flattened his nose against the glass of the window. He tried to make out the stations they were passing. But the numbers on the station signs were unexpected. Instead of Twenty-third Street, or Fourteenth Street, there were strange long numbers. The train was running more slowly now, and soon it became easier to read the numbers. There was less noise, too. Now John and Sarah could hear each other speak.

"That was *sixteen hundred ninety-five!*" cried John. "It sounds just like a date. Perhaps we've been back to the beginning of the world!"

"I hope we get back to today pretty soon!" Sarah cried.

But instead of reaching the present, they appeared to be going farther and farther back. *Sixteen hundred eighty-five* flashed past them. Then came *sixteen hundred sixty-four*.

"Say, that's the time when New York was still a Dutch town," said John, "when it was called New Amsterdam!"

"Well," said Sarah, "at least New Amsterdam won't be as crowded as New York is today!"

Suddenly she remembered. Her wish! Had *she* been standing on the magic spot when she made it?

The train swung round another curve, and Sarah leaned forward to look down its empty length. At that moment the lights in the farthest car began to grow dim. Then slowly, one by one, they went out. One car after another grew dark. Sarah clung to John's arm. He, too, was watching the darkness come closer. Then the lights above them became fainter, too.

The train was running more and more slowly now. Then as the very last light went out, it stopped. A great shiver ran through the train, as if it had run too far and too fast. *With a shudder — it broke into pieces!*

Sarah and John found themselves standing upon the track, too surprised to speak or to move.

Then John whispered, "Are you all right?"

"I think so," answered Sarah. She wasn't quite sure.

They looked at each other. Yes, they were both un-hurt. But what had happened?

All was quiet, and all was dark except for a little light that came from an opening far down the tunnel.

"Where are we?" whispered Sarah.

"That's to be seen," said John. "We've got to get out of here. Come on!"

He took her tightly by the arm, and the two started stumbling down the track toward the distant light.

In the Year 1664

Sᴀʀᴀʜ's ғᴏᴏᴛ ꜱʟɪᴘᴘᴇᴅ on a stone. She went down on her hands and knees. John pulled her quickly to her feet.

"Watch out where you step!" he warned, as though anyone could watch out in the dim light of the tunnel.

Sarah reached down to rub her knee. Something long and full got in her way. What could it be? She seemed to be wearing a long skirt. Then her foot hit another stone. As she hit it, there came a queer hollow, wooden sound. Sarah looked down at her feet in surprise, but she could see nothing in the darkness.

Then John, too, began to have trouble with his walking.

"I feel as if I had a house on each foot," he grumbled.

On and on went the two toward the distant light. At last John and Sarah reached the opening. In another minute they stepped out into bright sunlight. The sudden light blinded them. They stood blinking like two owls. When they could see again, they both gasped in amazement.

"Is it Florida or the North Pole?" cried Sarah.

"I'm sure I don't know!" John answered in bewilderment.

Bright-blue water stretched before them. Three boats rode at anchor not far from land. They were not like any boats that John or Sarah had ever seen before. They were sailing vessels, and they were gaily painted with pictures and designs.

The children turned slowly around. A high wall rose above their heads, and on the wall there were some cannon.

"It must be a fort," said Sarah. "I hope they don't fire those cannon," she added timidly.

"Well, this is neither Florida nor the North Pole. I'm sure of that," said John with decision. "But I'm not at all certain *where* we are!"

Around the fort stood a number of neat brick houses. They were homelike and cozy and gay. There were gardens and orchards behind them. The pointed roofs of the houses were toward the street. Some of them went up in steps. "Just like a staircase," said Sarah.

The street that led from house to house was cobbled with stones. A gutter ran down the middle of the street, and now down the gutter came a fat mother pig with five piglets. Suddenly the door of one of the little houses opened. Out came some refuse, thrown into the street. The mother pig grunted with pleasure. Then she and the little pigs began to eat noisily.

Just then Sarah noticed a windmill standing not far away. Its great arms were turning slowly.

"Why, John," she asked in surprise, "do you think we've gotten to Holland?"

She turned toward him, and at the same minute John turned to look at her. They stared at each other in astonishment. John no longer wore blue jeans and a striped T shirt. He had on baggy knee breeches and a short coat. On his legs were heavy hand-knit stockings, and on his feet were wooden shoes.

"Why, we're wearing Dutch clothes!" Sarah cried.

She spun round and round, so that her wide skirt flew out in a circle about her. Then she made a deep curtsy to John. But John was no longer watching her. He was looking carefully about him.

"You know," he said thoughtfully, "this place looks just like the end of Manhattan Island. There's New York Harbor, and there's Governor's Island out there where it ought to be. There's the Hudson River, and there's New Jersey over there where those trees are."

John was growing more and more excited. "Sarah," he cried, "we're right down where Battery Park ought to be. We're right where we meant to go all the time."

"But *where* are the high buildings and Brooklyn Bridge and the Statue of Liberty that you said we'd see?" asked Sarah all in one breath.

"This must be Dutch New York," said John slowly. "*Somehow or other we must have come back to the days when New York was New Amsterdam!*"

John began walking rapidly toward the windmill. "Come on, Sarah," he called. "Let's look this over first."

The two, in their wooden shoes, went clumping over to see the windmill.

"Everything seems so small when you know how New York looks today," said John. "This is just like a play town. That windmill is the tallest thing here, and I could throw a stone over it."

"I don't believe you could," said Sarah, just to tease him.

That was as good as a dare. John picked up a well-shaped stone and let it fly. It sailed up, and just cleared the top of the windmill. A lone sea gull on the rocks beyond rose crying and complaining into the air.

John turned with a smile to Sarah and said, "Now let's see *you* do it?"

Sarah frowned. She knew she couldn't. But she hated to admit it, so she picked up a stone and threw it as hard as she could. It landed with a bang against the wall of the mill.

John began to laugh, but suddenly the mill door swung open as though the stone had hit a hidden spring. Out popped the miller like a jack-in-the-box. He was a short fat man, and he was white as snow from head to foot from flour dust.

"What is it that you are doing, you two good-for-nothings?" he cried angrily. "You frighten a man out of his wits, you young rascals!"

The miller grew red in the face. He shook his fist

and came rapidly toward them. Sarah wanted to run, but John stood his ground.

Suddenly the whole town seemed to come to life. From out of the nearest houses came a dozen women all dressed in full dark skirts and white caps. Two of the women had their sleeves rolled up and held scrubbing brushes in their hands. Another one waved a long stocking that she was knitting. Another held a big black iron pot by the handle. One and all were talking as fast as they could, and talking all at once.

First they all scolded the miller. Indeed they soon seemed to have the better of him, for he turned and started back toward his mill, muttering.

"Very well, very well! Take care of your own children then," he grumbled. "But mind what I say! They'll come to no good!"

"There he goes, old crosspatch," laughed the woman who held the iron pot in her hand. "There he goes!"

Just then a plump pink-cheeked woman with soft yellow hair came running down the lane.

"Good day, Vrouw Hendricks, good day," called the other women. "Here is this pretty pair of rascals of yours. They were throwing stones at the miller. What are you going to do with them?"

"Dear, dear!" cried Vrouw Hendricks as she fanned herself with her apron. "Jan, why were you not digging the clams for the dinner? And, Sarah, my dear little Sarah, why were you not getting the fresh white sand to put on the floor? Why weren't you attending to your business, instead of playing pranks on poor old Derrick, the miller?"

But neither Sarah nor John could answer that question, and luckily the good vrouw did not stop to listen. Grasping each child by the hand, she walked ahead so vigorously that John and Sarah had to hurry to keep pace with her. Where were they going, they wondered? What was going to happen to them next?

They left the fort behind them and hurried along a country lane. They passed one house after another until they saw ahead a high plank wall which seemed to mark the end of the town. A wide gate in the wall stood open. Even as they hurried after Vrouw Hendricks, the children could catch a glimpse of the countryside beyond.

Vrouw Hendricks turned in at a neat little house. Here she plumped the children down on the doorstep and told them to wait.

Sarah and John sat looking at each other in surprise. "Who do you suppose we are?" Sarah was just asking when Vrouw Hendricks came back.

"Here," she said, "take these and be off with you, my dears!"

John found that he held a wooden pail and a wooden shovel. Sarah had a bag and a little wooden scoop. But they did not have time to look at them long, for Vrouw Hendricks was pushing them toward the gate in the wall and telling them to mind what they did this time. Just as she gave them a final push, out came her hand from behind her apron. There were two large sugared friedcakes, still warm and fresh. Sarah and John tasted the cakes very carefully. Then they almost gobbled them up. They were delicious!

"Now away with you," the good Vrouw said with a laugh.

Sarah and John ran out through the gate in the wall.

At first they came to fields and pastures. Beyond these rose low wooded hills, where the forest began. A well-worn path led down to the water's edge. Sarah and John followed it. As they went, they ate the last delicious crumbs of friedcake.

"Well," said John at length, "so it appears that we are Dutch. That's interesting. Won't our mothers be surprised!"

"Yes, they will," said Sarah softly.

The mention of her mother made her feel a little queer. Then a sudden thought came to her.

"Why, John!" she cried. "They were talking Dutch, and we understood what they said. They understood us. We must be talking Dutch, too." Sarah ran her tongue round the inside of her mouth. "But I don't feel anything different," she said.

"Silly!" said John. "The language you talk doesn't feel different inside your mouth! But what's worrying me now is how are we going to get any clams?"

"Oh, I know how!" cried Sarah, who was delighted to know something that John did not know. "I dug clams when I went to Nantucket last summer. You find them in the mud when the tide goes out. A little bubble of air shows where each one is. Come on."

Everything but clams was forgotten. The two ran quickly down to the shore and began their search.

"Here you are," Sarah called.

She stopped where a little bubble of air was forcing its way up through the mud. John dug quickly down through the ooze. Out came a clam, looking at them a little reproachfully. John dumped it into his bucket.

"Clams for sale! Clams for sale!" chanted Sarah as she snatched up the bucket.

"You've found only one, Sarah," said John sternly. "We've a great deal more work to do before you begin shouting."

They began walking along the shore. Now and again they added a clam to their pail. Now and again they stopped to dig a little lake and watch it fill with water. Then they caught two crabs and raced them against each other.

At last the pail was filled. It had grown very heavy. John looked around for a safe place, well back from the water, where he could leave it. He decided to put it under a tree in the forest. The forest came down to the shore. John and Sarah were out of sight of house or farm by now. All signs of town had by now been left behind.

"Now that's done," said Sarah with pleasure, "but the next question is, how am I going to find my sand? There is nothing but mud here."

"Perhaps we can find some up the shore a little way," said John.

He was glad to be free of his pail and to be able to wander along the shore. A rocky ledge lay just ahead of them. They began to climb over it, but it was hard to climb in wooden shoes. Soon they had their shoes off and were carrying them. They walked on and on;

it was fun to see what lay beyond the next curve.

When Sarah grew tired, they stopped to make a little pool in the sand. They caught some starfish and some snails to put in the pool. They collected sea-weed. They went wading in the shallow water.

Sarah and John had quite forgotten that they had gone back three hundred years in as many minutes! They forgot that where they were playing there should have been great docks and tall office buildings and factories. They thought only of what fun it was to be at the seashore on an August day.

At last they came to the mouth of a little stream. Here they found the white sand that Sarah needed to fill her bag.

"Now that's done," said Sarah. "Nobody will scold us."

She sat down on a rock with her feet in the water. Suddenly she jumped up with a cry. She had laid her wooden shoes down on the beach. Now quietly but surely the waves were carrying them off!

John splashed out after the shoes. He caught one, but the other went sailing off like a little boat.

"Get me a stick," he called.

Sarah snatched up a branch and handed it to John. He fished for the runaway, but it was useless. Off went the shoe, rising and falling easily on the waves.

"Oh, well," said Sarah, "I never did think much of those wooden shoes. I'll get on as well barefoot. The only thing I want is something to eat. It's been a long time since breakfast."

John felt in his pockets. Luckily he found a whole bar of chocolate, and they ate it with relish. Then they followed the little brook into the woods until its water was fresh enough to drink. It was such fun to wade in the brook that they went on and on until they could no longer hear the lapping of the waves on the shore.

At last they came out of the dim forest into a little clearing in the wood. There was a thick, soft carpet of moss on the ground. John kicked off his shoes and dug his bare toes into the moss.

But Sarah had found some blackberries. At once they pounced upon them. When they'd had their fill of berries, they lay down on the moss. It was pleasant to look up through the leaves of the tall trees above them. Squirrels played in the branches and dropped acorns on their heads. A rabbit hopped out from the brambles and nibbled at Sarah's hand.

John and Sarah rested on the thick moss, tired and happy. They both dozed a little. Slowly the sun moved across the sky above them.

Five
Musket
Shots

B O-O-OM — BO-O-OM — BO-O-OM. The noise shook the ground. John and Sarah jumped up in alarm. Was it thunder? But the sun was still shining, although the shadows across the little clearing were growing long.

BO-O-OM — BO-O-OM — BO-O-OM. Again came the deep roars. Three times.

"It must be the cannon — the cannon on the fort we saw," cried John. "I wish I were there to see it go off!"

"I'm glad I'm not," said Sarah with much feeling.

"Maybe the Indians are attacking," went on John, "or maybe —"

He did not finish, for again there came the loud BO-O-OM. This time there were answering shots. They were the smaller *bo-o-oms* of muskets. And the sounds came from a spot not far from where John and Sarah were standing.

"Come along! Quick!" John said. "We'd better hide."

"Where?" answered Sarah, whose heart seemed to be doing a war dance inside her.

Again they heard shooting. This time they could hear men shouting and calling to one another.

"They're coming this way," whispered John. "Follow me!"

They ran into the forest, but they could not go far or fast. Their way was blocked by briers, underbrush, vines, and fallen trees. In a very few minutes Sarah's bare foot was scratched and bruised. She was almost in tears.

Then John found an old oak tree that had been blown down in a winter storm. He climbed onto the great trunk and pulled Sarah up after him. A thick tangle of grapevines had grown over the branches of the tree. The children crept along the trunk until they reached a hiding place in a cave of green leaves. They crouched down in the branches of the old tree, and the grapevines closed about them. They were hidden from sight.

More shots resounded through the woods. A frightened deer came crashing through the underbrush. It stopped for a moment, not sure which way to turn. Cries and shouts now came from every direction. Then a volley of shots came from the north, and the deer fled to the south.

"Do you think Indians are attacking everywhere all at once?" whispered Sarah in dismay.

"Hush!" warned John. He could hear footsteps. "Keep perfectly still!"

In another minute three men with guns over their shoulders came into the clearing. They wore heavy dark clothing and wide felt hats. They seemed troubled and worried, and they looked anxiously about them as they crossed the clearing.

Then there were more shouts. "Ho-there! Yo-ho!" They seemed to be coming from the shore.

"It sounds as if they'd found something," one man said hopefully. "Come on!"

"I hope it's something besides a little wooden shoe this time," said a second man. His face was sad and grave.

"Come on," cried the first one. "Let's find out what it is."

The three men hurried down the trail. Through the leaves the children watched them go. Then they looked at each other, wondering what was going to happen next.

Suddenly John gripped Sarah's arm, and pointed to the far side of the clearing. A tall Indian had stepped out of the wood. He stood all alone, looking about him. Sarah's heart seemed to stand still. Then it started again, thumping like an engine inside her.

The copper-brown skin of the Indian shone in the late-afternoon light. He was naked except for a fur at his waist, and the quiver of arrows that hung from his shoulder. His hair stood up in a straight black ruff. A band held two feathers in place.

For a moment the Indian stood like a statue. Then he looked about him carefully. He seemed to notice every bush and stick and stone in the clearing. Then quietly he walked down the trail where the white men had gone. Not a stick cracked. Not a leaf stirred. Before the children realized it, he had vanished.

Sarah pressed close to John. Neither spoke a word. They both listened and waited.

After a while the light in their green hiding place

began to grow dim. Mosquitoes came out and began to hum around them. It seemed as if they had been there for hours.

All at once, for some reason, John thought of his mother. He bit his lip. This was just the sort of mess that she would blame him for getting Sarah into! Sarah would probably be in tears next. Girls were like that! And what would he do then?

As for Sarah, she felt afraid and lonely. It was all so strange. Of one thing Sarah was sure, though. She was not going to cry if she could help it. She was not going to make matters worse for John.

The vines above the children began to move slightly. Was it an evening breeze or some animal? Sarah held her breath and sat up very straight. John leaned forward ready to do his best whatever might happen.

Again the vines stirred. Then, very carefully and slowly, the leaves were parted. The children peered up through the opening. They looked straight into the face of the Indian, who was gazing intently at them.

It was almost more than Sarah could bear. She fought back the tears. One sob rose to her throat, but she gulped it down.

Then the copper-brown face disappeared as suddenly as it had come. A shrill whistle sounded long and clear. It was repeated again and again. Was he calling a band of Indian braves to take them prisoners? The sound of running steps was heard. They were not the silent footfalls of Indians trained to the woods. They were the *thud, thud, thud* of stout boots. Cries and shouts echoed through the woods.

All at once Sarah realized what the men were calling. "They're found! They're found!" came the shouts. "Yo-ho there!"

Again the Indian pushed back the leaves that hid the children. This time he stooped and picked up Sarah. She was too surprised to say anything as he carried her gently into the clearing. John followed close behind.

"Found! Found!" came the shouts through the woods. "The children are found! Safe and alive!"

"*Why* — " gasped John in amazement, "*were they looking for us?*"

In a few minutes there were twenty or thirty men gathered about the children. Sarah was caught up in strong arms and hugged and kissed. John was patted on the back and hugged as well. There was talking and laughing. Everyone was so glad to find the children that no one stopped to listen to them.

"My little Sarah! My little Sarah!" one man kept saying. "First we found the bucket of clams, and then we found the bag of sand. Then Gerrit brought in your shoe, your little wooden shoe. We thought you had been drowned. We dared not take it home to your mother!"

"It was wildcats that I feared the most, Mynheer Hendricks," cried another man. "I dared not say it, but I feared that wildcats had gotten them! They're dangerous animals. There's nothing worse on the Island of Manhattan than a wildcat. It climbs out on the branch of a tree and drops on a man as he rests. A man can do nothing against one, much less a boy and a little girl. Thank Heaven no wildcat found them!"

There was so much talk that it was some time before John could make himself heard. "But aren't the Indians attacking us?" he asked. "Why was there shooting?"

"Indians attacking?" cried Mynheer Hendricks. "Is that what you thought? Is that why you were hiding? Oh, no! There's fighting up the river, but not here, God be praised! The shooting that you heard was the alarm. On all sides men have been hunting for you. The Director General, Peter Stuyvesant himself, ordered the cannon to be fired. He is a firm man, but he has a heart. He has children of his own."

"It was Temaquoy, the Indian tracker, who found you," said another man. "It takes the eye of an Indian to see what no one else can see."

"But come now," cried still another man, "we must signal to the town that all is well. Vrouw Hendricks has been crying her eyes out all the afternoon."

Five guns were loaded from powder horns that hung at the men's belts. When the five were ready, Mynheer Hendricks gave the signal. Sarah longed to put her hands over her ears. Then she remembered that she was not going to disgrace John.

Five shots were fired into the air. Birds perched in the trees went crying through the woods in alarm. When the last echoes had died away, one BO-O-OM came in answer from the fort. Then all was quiet.

Now back to the town went the band of searchers. A trail led through the woods by the side of the brook. It was growing dark, and the men walked quickly to make as much use as possible of the fading light. One man carried Sarah on his shoulder. Mynheer Hendricks led John by the hand.

Finally they left the dusk of the woods, and came out again among the fields and orchards. The last of the sunset glowed in the sky. Windows in the little houses ahead were already lighted.

At the gate in the wall, a crowd of women were waiting. The children were hugged and kissed all over again. Again no one stopped to listen to anything they said. It was just as well. Neither John nor Sarah had the slightest idea what to say. It was far easier not to try to explain — just to let themselves be taken lovingly home.

The little house looked very cozy and inviting to the two tired children. A fire burned in the big fireplace that filled one end of the room. Above it hung a big kettle. From the ceiling hung a brass chandelier filled with lighted candles. On the wall were copper pans polished so brightly that Sarah could see her reflection in them. She was surprised to see the white cap on top of her dark hair. She had forgotten her Dutch clothes.

The children sat on low stools before the fire. Vrouw Hendricks filled two blue bowls with hot soup. The soup and big pieces of bread tasted so good! They were hungry as bears.

Neighbors kept dropping in. Many children gathered around the fire. Some seemed to belong to Vrouw Hendricks. Some seemed to have come to stare at

John and Sarah. Vrouw Hendricks hurried about, seeing that all were made welcome and comfortable.

Suddenly there was a stir outside the house. A loud *tap, tap, tap* sounded on the stone steps.

"It's the Director General," voices cried. "It's the Governor himself!"

Everyone in the room rose to his feet except Sarah and John, who were too surprised to move. Vrouw Hendricks hurried forward. She bobbed and curtsied up and down. "Come in, come in, Your Excellency," she kept saying.

A tall dark figure stood in the doorway. He wore a wide felt hat. A long dark cape covered his figure. He held a cane in one hand, and Sarah and John could see that he had only one leg. In place of the other was a wooden leg with bands of gleaming silver around it.

"Why — why, it's Peter Stuyvesant!" whispered John to Sarah. "You know about him, don't you? He's the Dutch governor with the wooden leg!" John and Sarah stared at him with round eyes. Then they suddenly remembered their manners and rose quickly to their feet. John made a bow, and Sarah bobbed her best curtsy.

"Good evening, Mynheer Hendricks and Vrouw Hendricks," said the Governor in a low, deep voice.

"My greetings to you. It is a blessing indeed that the children are safe and at home again!"

"Thank you, thank you, Your Excellency," cried Vrouw Hendricks as she curtsied again. "Pray be seated."

She pushed forward a tall carved chair with a leather seat and back.

"I can stay but a few minutes," said Governor Stuyvesant. Then he turned to John and asked the very question that John had been afraid that someone would ask. "*How did it happen, my son?*"

Now John could not very well say, "*We started out this morning on the subway. By mistake we ran back nearly three hundred years and landed in New Amsterdam. We were so surprised and excited that we wandered along the shore and never thought about the time.*" John could not very well say that. He could think of nothing else to say, but luckily his mother spoke for him.

"The lad is heedless, Your Excellency," she cried. "There is no harm in him, but he is headstrong and heedless. The boy took the wrong path by mistake and lost his way in the woods. But see what good care he took of Sarah! Will you believe it, I do not think she has even cried."

The Governor turned to John. The boy thought that he saw a twinkle in the great man's eyes. Then Stuyvesant's face became stern again.

"Well, my son," he said slowly, "see to it that tomorrow you stay at home and do a little work, by *mistake*."

The Governor turned to talk with Mynheer Hendricks. John gave Sarah a quick glance. Then the two of them sat listening, quietly trying to understand what it was all about. It was strange talk to their ears.

"Things are not going well in New Amsterdam," said one of the men. "The Indians are fighting again up the Great River." Sarah shuddered. Then another man went on, "But it is the English who are giving us the most trouble. They are very bad neighbors to the Dutch. They are making much trouble on Long Island. The Dutch West India Company is supposed to be managing the affairs of our New Amsterdam, but I must say it has done little to help us. We have few guns, little gunpowder, few soldiers in the fort, and no money for more." So the talk went.

Sarah could understand very little of what the men were talking about. She looked at the picture on the blue tiles that lined the fireplace, but she could not keep her eyes open. Soon her head began to nod. Vrouw Hendricks picked her up in her strong arms and carried her off to bed. But John sat listening to the men. He longed to ask questions, but he did not dare.

At last Governor Stuyvesant rose and wished them all good night. There were more bows and curtsies. A servant with a lantern in which one candle burned lighted the way for His Excellency. Then the door was closed behind him.

"Think of it!" cried Vrouw Hendricks. "Just fancy His Excellency coming himself to see that all was well with the children! Ah well, he's had children of his own. He knows how a parent feels. But fancy him coming himself!"

"Fancy it indeed," thought John to himself. "Who would ever have fancied seeing Peter Stuyvesant!"

"But now to bed," went on Vrouw Hendricks as she bent over the fire, covering the burning coals with ashes. "Now to bed, for we must be up with the sun. Such a day as it's been!"

"There has never been such a one before," thought John. But he said it only to himself.

A Day in New Amsterdam

THE NEXT DAY was anything but dull for John and Sarah.

Vrouw Hendricks let the children sleep late. She herself was up before sunrise, to be ready for the herdsman who came for the cows. Faintly in his dreams John heard the horn of the herdsman coming closer and closer as he went from house to house. He could hear voices far away, "Are the cows ready for pasture?" "Yes, they are. Watch them well lest wolves get them or they stray into the woods!"

As the herdsman reached the Hendricks' gate, John was just awake enough to hear him talking with Vrouw Hendricks. As if in a dream, John heard the herdsman say, "Good day, Vrouw Hendricks, and how are the children? It's dreadful indeed to think of them lost in the woods on this Island of Manhattan."

He heard Vrouw Hendricks reply, "The children are sleeping late. I shall not waken them until seven o'clock, or perhaps not until eight. They need rest. Watch out that that brindled cow doesn't get into my garden."

"Hi, there," shouted the herdsman.

John turned over, still not really awake, "Cows on the streets of New York! It must be something on the radio," he thought drowsily. Then he went back to sleep.

The sun was high in the sky before John and Sarah were finally awake and dressed. "I slept in a cupboard," Sarah told John when they met. "You know, there was a great big featherbed in it as soft as a cloud."

"My bed rolled out from under a big one," said John. "I don't know what I slept on. I was too tired.

I'm hungry as a wolf now. Have you had breakfast?"

Vrouw Hendricks gave them bread and cheese and milk. "It's so near dinnertime, you don't need much," she said.

As soon as they had finished eating, she called them to help her with the cooking.

"Now Sarah," she said as she came bustling out of the pantry, "you may turn the spit, and mind you do it carefully."

Sarah opened her eyes wide in surprise. "Turn the — the — the — what?" she asked.

"Why, whatever is the matter with the child?" cried Vrouw Hendricks. "Has one day in the woods turned her wits? See, here it is all ready, with a fine fat turkey on it. You'll not have forgotten how to eat turkey, I'm sure."

Before the fire stood an open oven. Inside hung a large turkey speared on an iron rod. There was a handle at one end of the rod so that the turkey could be turned round and round. "Now see to it that it is well browned on all sides," said Vrouw Hendricks, who was an excellent cook and housewife.

With much interest, Sarah and John knelt down by the turkey. They began to turn the handle of the spit carefully.

" 'Tis a fine bird," said the good woman as she looked at it proudly. "I bought it from an Indian for a string of wampum and six brass bells. Fancy wanting little brass bells! These Indians are strange people. I can never get used to them. But then there is no way of telling *what* people will fancy!"

Vrouw Hendricks went back into her pantry. The children began to turn the turkey. Without thinking what they were doing, they turned it faster and faster.

Juices flew out and sizzled on the hot coals. Back ran Vrouw Hendricks in alarm.

"What are you two doing?" she cried. "Spinning the turkey like a top? Turn it slowly and evenly! You two seem to have bewitched each other. One is enough to mind the spit. Sarah, you come with me."

So John was left alone with the turkey. "I wonder what she'd think if I told her about gas stoves and electric ovens and all those things," he thought.

In the pantry Sarah found a new surprise awaiting her. She was told to churn the cream into butter, and she was given a queer-looking little barrel with a pole sticking out of it. She had to climb up on a stool to reach the pole which Vrouw Hendricks called the "dasher." Sarah found it hard work to pump the dasher up and down, and twirl it around. She bit her lip, and her face grew red and hot, but she worked away at it.

The more Sarah worked, the harder and harder the work became. At last she could scarcely move the dasher at all. All at once Vrouw Hendricks saw what was happening.

"Child, child!" she cried. "Don't you know enough to stop churning when the butter's come?"

Then she noticed how hot and tired Sarah looked.

"But you've done it beautifully," she said. "See."

Vrouw Hendricks poured off the buttermilk and then took out the soft, fresh butter. She washed it and packed it into a jar. Sarah rested her tired arms and watched. It certainly was butter — real butter. Suddenly she was quite proud of herself.

Meanwhile the little servingmaid who helped Vrouw Hendricks was setting the long table. She spread it with a fresh white cloth, and at each place put a napkin and a spoon and knife. Then she pulled up the benches and stools and chairs. Sarah and John watched her with interest.

"How many of us do you suppose there are?" whispered Sarah to John.

There was a delicious smell from the turkey, which was nearly done. It seemed to draw the Hendricks family as a magnet draws iron. In they all came! First came three boys, one larger and two smaller than John. He soon found out they were Kilian, Nicholas, and Gerrit. Each boy brought in something — water or different vegetables from the garden. As he entered the house, each boy left his wooden shoes outside the door and put on felt slippers. Each spoke politely to Vrouw Hendricks as he entered, and each washed his hands before he came for his dinner.

Vrouw Hendricks had a warm smile and a greeting for each.

Then came Mynheer Hendricks and his younger brother, who, it seemed, had but recently come from Holland. The two men sat down at the head of the table. Then there was laughing and calling and joking as the oldest sister, Catelina, brought in the twins, Annetka and Lysbet. They were only two years old and the pets of the family. Each was lifted into a high chair. Sarah thought they looked like two golden-haired Dutch dolls — very hungry dolls, for they beat on the table and could scarcely wait for food.

At last came the grandmother, who sat by Vrouw Hendricks. Now the family was complete. John and Sarah looked about with interest. There were four children at each side of the table.

"*Eight children!*" murmured John to Sarah, who sat beside him. "Do you know, that's what my mother always said she wanted! But there's only room for me in our apartment."

The dinner smelled very good indeed. Sarah and John were quite ready for it. But they were to have no food for some time yet.

When all the children were seated, Mynheer Hendricks rose very solemnly. He took a big Bible from the cupboard behind the table. Slowly he opened it and found his place. Slowly and carefully he wiped a pair of large glasses in a heavy steel frame. He placed them upon his nose. Then he began to read aloud. On and on he went. It was hard for Sarah to sit still. She wiggled a little, but John pinched her under the table, and she sat up very straight again and held herself very still.

One of the twins began to whimper, but Catelina gave each a little lump of brown sugar to keep them quiet. When the reading was over and the big Bible laid away, a prayer began. In a grave, quiet voice Mynheer Hendricks gave thanks for his family and his comfortable home in this new land, and for the food that was soon to be on the table.

When it was over, something happened that surprised John. He could hardly believe his eyes. Solemnly Mynheer Hendricks put his big felt hat upon his head and sat down at his place. Mynheer's brother did the same, and so did the boys. On went all the hats. John reached quickly for his hat and clapped it on his head. If that was the way things were done in New Amsterdam, all well and good. He did not want to be different. What he wanted was turkey!

Sarah could hardly keep from giggling as she peeked at John. He had pulled his hat down over his nose, and was trying to look as serious as Mynheer Hendricks himself. But now the hot dishes were being brought to the table, and everything else was forgotten.

The first food served was a big bowl of mashed peas cooked with ginger and butter. It had a strange taste, but Sarah and John rather liked it. Then came clams and lobster. At last came the turkey, with turnips and greens to go with it. Pewter plates were filled again and again.

While the family ate, the little servingmaid stood by the table, brushing away the flies. It was late August, and there were many flies about. Sarah noticed with surprise that there were no screens in the windows. "I don't suppose screens have been invented yet," she thought. "Just think of that!"

The outside door was divided across the middle, making an upper and lower door. The day was warm, and the door stood wide open. Vrouw Hendricks shut the lower half as she drove out the dog and two cats, but there was nothing to keep out the buzzing, hungry flies. The little maid was busy with her fan, but even so there were many on the table. A few wasps joined them, but the family paid no attention. No one talked much as they ate.

It was John who first broke the silence. The next minute he wished very much that he had not spoken. John could find only a spoon and knife at his place, so without thinking he asked, "May I please have a fork?"

Everyone stopped eating and stared at John in amazement. John turned very red.

"A *fork?*" cried Mynheer Hendricks. "*A fork!* Not even His Excellency has a fork! Does the boy think that because he's been lost in the woods for a day he should eat like the King of England? There's not a fork in New Amsterdam."

John wished that he could sink through the floor to cover his confusion, but Vrouw Hendricks saved the day for him.

"The boy will have his jokes," she laughed. "Fancy his even thinking to ask for a fork! There are not many boys his age who even know what a fork is!"

This time it was very hard indeed for Sarah to keep from laughing. She bent over one of the twins to hide her face. When she turned back, she was glad to see that the family had all begun to eat again. She did not dare look at John. She cut up her meat with her knife and ate it with her fingers. When she did glance in John's direction, he had a drumstick in his hand and was doing quite nicely with no fork.

After the turkey was eaten, there were almond cakes and jelly tarts and fruit. Vrouw Hendricks sat and smiled with pleasure as the good things disappeared. "In winter it is hard to get all the good things that my family like," she said, "but now, at the end of summer, there are delicacies aplenty."

When dinner was over, John and Sarah sat back, well filled with good things. But they soon found there was to be no rest for them. In New Amsterdam everyone worked. Everyone was assigned a task but the twins, who were to take their naps like good babies. John was to weed in the garden. Sarah was to spin.

Sarah cast a look of despair toward John as he went out the door, but there was no help from him! Then she walked to the spinning wheel. What was she to do? It was a wheel for spinning wool, and was higher than she was tall. Sarah gave the big wheel a turn. Round and round it spun. She gave a pull at the mop of unspun wool on the spindle. In a few minutes everything was in a tangle.

Vrouw Hendricks cried out, "Sarah child, I can't make out what has come over you! I must have let you run wild too long with John. One day in the woods, and you are a savage!"

Then she saw Sarah's face. "Never you mind, child," she exclaimed. "I'll help you spin later. Here, take the twins for a walk. They don't seem to be able to sleep as they should. You mind them for me. Go to Vrouw van der Grift's cottage and get me the fine linen she has bleached for me. I hope you remember it's the last cottage at end of the lane, the one with the thatched roof."

Sarah was very glad to leave the spinning and to start down the lane. She held the two fat, rosy Dutch babies each by a small plump hand. They were well-fed, comfortable babies, and gave her little trouble.

Vrouw van der Grift was well known in New Amsterdam for her fine spinning and weaving. No one could spin so fine a thread as she. No one could weave so close a cloth. Her great chest was filled with sheets and tablecloths and rolls of linen. It was the wonder of all the housewives. No one in town could equal it.

When Sarah and the twins reached the thatched cottage, they found Vrouw van der Grift at her wheel. They stood and watched her. *Whrr-rr*, round went the wheel, and the little old lady's hands flew back and forth as she spun the flax to a thin, strong thread. She smiled a welcome to the three children.

But in another minute there were four instead of three, for John joined them. He had seen Sarah pass by the garden where he was working. He was tired of weeding and had decided to take a little vacation. In a few minutes Vrouw van der Grift stopped her wheel. She took the children into her cottage, gave them sweet cakes to eat, and showed them her big white cat. The twins were delighted, but the cat kept well out of their way.

"And now," said the little old lady, "you must see my *kas*, my big linen chest that came from Holland."

The big chest stood in a little hall off the tiny kitchen. The hall was lighted by a little window in the wall above the chest. That window had more than one use. As Vrouw van der Grift stood smiling, the white cat jumped to the top of the *kas* and went out the window. Vrouw van der Grift laughed.

"That's his way of getting in and out," she said. "I always call that the cat's window. He is not sure he likes the twins. He's afraid they'll pull his tail."

Then Vrouw van der Grift opened the doors of the chest. It was filled to overflowing with her precious linen.

"See how fine this is!" she cried. "It's even fine enough for His Excellency's shirts. I spun and wove every bit of it myself. And see, here are fifty sheets, twenty tablecloths, and a hundred napkins."

It sounded like a whole linen shop to Sarah. In amazement, she asked, "Why do you want so many? You can't use them."

Now it was John's turn to laugh at Sarah's mistake. The little old lady turned to her in astonishment.

"Why do I want so many?" she cried. "Never was such a question asked in New Amsterdam or in old Amsterdam! Every good housewife must have her *kas* well filled. The more linen the better. Whatever are you thinking of!"

Sarah had just time to murmur politely. "The linen is beautiful, I'm sure. It's very, very nice!" She stopped talking, for the big white cat had come back through the window mewing. He held a little gray mouse in his mouth.

Vrouw van der Grift did not want a mouse in her nice clean house. "Go away! Take it away!" she scolded, and she ran for the broom made of twigs that stood by the fireplace. The twins laughed and crowed, and held up their plump little hands for the cat. That was enough for the cat. He turned, and out the window he went again! The twins sent up cries of disappointment.

Sarah decided that it was time for them to start for home. She picked up the package of linen that Vrouw Vander Grift had ready for her and thanked the little old lady for her kindness. Then she started home with the twins.

John walked beside Sarah. "Think of her having all that linen," said Sarah softly. "What can she do with it?"

"Well," said John, "the Indians want little brass bells and the Dutch seem to want linen. As Vrouw Hendricks says, 'There's no way of telling what people will fancy.'"

But now the twins were tired. They sat down on a doorstep and refused to go any farther. There was nothing for Sarah and John to do but pick them up. So Sarah took one of them pickaback, and John took the other. In a minute the twins were happy and gay again. Down the lane they all went merrily.

When they reached home, they found Mynheer Hendricks and Vrouw Hendricks and several of the children in the garden under a big tree. They were eating cakes and fruit and chatting together. The twins were soon drinking milk out of bright silver mugs that had come from Holland. Sarah and John were resting on the grass, eating juicy peaches.

When he finished his peach, John tried a dangerous experiment. Mynheer Hendricks was smoking his pipe. John glanced up at him. Mynheer Hendricks looked ready for a talk, and John decided to ask questions.

"What do you think it will be like, here on Manhattan Island," asked John, "in the years to come?"

Mynheer took his long slender pipe out of his mouth and blew the smoke into the air. "I don't think that the town will grow much larger," he said gravely. "It is large enough now."

John glanced at Sarah mischievously, and then he went on. "Do you think there will ever be high buildings, built right here, where this very house stands today? Buildings that will go up into the air fifty or sixty stories high?"

"Nonsense!" said Mynheer Hendricks, and he blew more smoke into the air. "The Town Hall is four stories high, and that is as tall as any building will ever be on Manhattan Island, you may be sure."

Sarah sent a warning look toward John, but the boy went on. He had to choose his words carefully. He could not mention elevators or automobiles or electricity, or even trains, for Mynheer Hendricks would not even know what the words meant.

"Do you think," began John with a twinkle in his eye, "that there will ever be carriages, on these very streets, that will run by themselves with no horses to pull them? Do you think that perhaps there will ever be lights, with no fire burning in them, that will light up the whole house by just pressing a button?"

Mynheer Hendricks sat up and looked sharply at the boy, but John did not realize his danger. He went right on. "Do you suppose that someone will invent something that will send messages across the ocean to Holland? Or a machine that will fly around the world?"

John got no further. He had said enough and too much. Mynheer Hendricks was sitting up very straight and growing red in the face.

"Has the boy lost his wits?" he cried. "He should be put to bed. He must have a fever!"

"There, there," said Vrouw Hendricks comfortingly. "I'll brew him some herb tea. He is tired. Yesterday was too much for him."

So John was promptly put to bed! Vrouw Hendricks stood over him while he drank a great big bowl of hot bitter tea. Sarah peeked in at him, and he made faces as he drank it. But Vrouw Hendricks saw to it that every drop went down. It was Sarah's turn to laugh, but she was careful not to let Vrouw Hendricks see her. There was more herb tea in the kettle!

As Vrouw Hendricks tucked John in for the night, she said something that made both children forget herb tea. "You'll be quite all right for school in the morning," she said.

"*School in the morning!*" repeated John and Sarah together. "Why, it's only August!"

"Why not in August?" asked Vrouw Hendricks. "You've had three days vacation because the master was away. Now he's back. We have school every month in the year now, and I'm proud of it."

"It's nothing to be proud of," muttered John as she left him.

Sarah waited until Vrouw Hendricks was out of earshot. "John," she whispered, "don't you think we ought to search for the entrance to that tunnel tomorrow?"

"I *have* looked," John answered. "I've looked and looked, but I haven't found a trace of it. Don't you worry though, I'll find it yet!"

FIRE!
FIRE!

Bᴜᴛ next morning there was no hunting for tunnels.

The next morning everyone was up at sunrise. There were many tasks to be done before school began at eight. Breakfast was so early that John and Sarah were almost too sleepy to eat, but no one seemed to notice.

After breakfast there was wood to be brought in for the fire. There were dishes to be washed and the floor to be scrubbed. There was brass and copper to be polished till it shone like the sun. At last the four oldest children were through with their work and ready to start for school. Off went Kilian and Catelina, and Sarah and John followed them to the schoolhouse.

The sky was blue and the day clear. It seemed a shame to have to stay indoors. The school was held in one room of the master's house. It was quite different from the large light schoolrooms that Sarah and John were used to. The ceiling was low, and the room was hot and close.

"Oh, dear!" sighed Sarah as she looked about her. "I don't like this at all."

John and Sarah watched the other children entering the schoolroom. Each went to say good morning to the master, who sat at a high desk. Then each child stood before him and recited the morning prayer while the master listened carefully, to be sure that every word was just exactly right.

"What are we going to do?" whispered Sarah anxiously to John as they waited for their turn.

"I don't know *what* to say to him!" said John. "Do you think he'll put me in the corner and make me wear a duncecap?" The prayer was quite a different one from any John or Sarah had ever heard before.

Luckily, just then several more children arrived. It was growing late, so the master had them all say the prayer together. John and Sarah repeated what the others said. Sarah gave a sigh of relief. That was over! What would happen next?

There were only long benches without backs for the children to sit on. All the girls sat on one side of the room and all the boys on the other. The boys kept their hats on. At first Sarah could hardly keep from laughing when she looked at John. He sat so straight on the hard bench and he looked so businesslike. But school, when it began, was no laughing matter. Sarah soon found that out!

First all the children sang a psalm. Then the master read from the Bible. On and on and on he went until Sarah grew very tired. Before she knew what she was doing, she gave a great yawn. The master stopped reading and looked at her severely.

"Sarah Hendricks," he said, "you are not listening to the word of Our Lord. Stand here by my side."

Sarah grew very red as she went to his desk. The other children began to laugh, but the master rapped sharply for silence. The reading continued. Sarah stood first on one foot and then on the other until it was over. At last she was sent back to her seat.

Next, each class stood in a row and read aloud in turn. John and Sarah found the books very dull. Luckily they could read as well as most of the children, so no one paid special attention to them. They were glad of that.

Then the older classes had writing. Each child had a gray goose quill cut to a sharp point. John found it fun to write with a quill pen. He tried writing a number of different things. Then he wrote in large letters: "I LIVE IN NEW YORK CITY, NEW YORK STATE, THE UNITED STATES OF AMERICA."

Just then the master passed by. "What's this? What's this?" he cried. "Wasting paper and writing nonsense! Who ever heard of *New York City!* There's no such place."

John was afraid he was going to grow even more angry, but suddenly the master looked at the clock.

"Put away your writing," he ordered. "It's past time for me to hear you say the Catechism, the Ten Commandments, and the Confession of Sin. The Domine will test you next Sunday. We have no time to lose."

On and on and on went the drill. It seemed to Sarah as though it would never stop. She grew more and more tired.

"Careful," whispered Catelina, who sat next to

her, "if you don't work harder than this, you'll fail next Sunday."

"Dear, dear," sighed Sarah, and she did her best to pay attention to all the master said.

At eleven o'clock there were more prayers, another hymn, and then at last the children were told to go home.

"Be back promptly at one," warned the master sternly.

There was a great clatter of wooden shoes as the children rushed eagerly into the street. Sarah and John followed behind the others.

"It's a dreadful school," began Sarah. "No painting or drawing — "

"No shop or gym," John added.

"No recess and no assembly," went on Sarah.

"No science," said John. "And you have to go all summer as well as all winter."

It was dreadful to consider. By the time John and Sarah reached home, their spirits were very low indeed. But the smell of dinner cheered them up. They hastened into the little house.

"Sarah and John!" cried Vrouw Hendricks in dismay. "What are you two doing, walking on my clean floor with your shoes on!"

The two children stopped short and looked at their feet. Then they slipped quickly through the door. They kicked off their wooden shoes and left them on the stoop. They put on their felt slippers and went quietly to their places at the table. They were ready, and more than ready, for one of Vrouw Hendricks' good meals. If only for a few minutes they could forget there was school again that afternoon.

When the meal was over and the children could eat no more, they sat back comfortably. "Oh," sighed Sarah, "why do the hands of the clock on the wall have to turn so quickly?" She could not bear the thought of more school. Suddenly the loud ticking of the clock was lost in the noise of shouting in the street outside.

"What can they be shouting about?" asked Vrouw Hendricks in surprise. "Have the cows run away, or has a ship come from Holland? I never heard such goings-on!"

Sarah and John ran to the door. The cries grew louder and louder. People were running and shouting. At last the words they were crying became frightfully clear. FIRE! FIRE!

The entire Hendricks family jumped to their feet. Out the door they went as fast as they could go. The

men and boys ran on ahead. The girls came next.
Vrouw Hendricks and Catelina followed, each carrying a twin.

Everyone else in New Amsterdam seemed to be
running in the same direction. Dogs began barking
noisily. Pigs squealed and ran, frightened, out of people's way. In the distance there was a red glow against
the sky, and toward that red glow everyone ran.

The house that was burning was at the far end of
the street near the East River. As Sarah and John
drew near to it, they saw which one it was. "It's the
thatched cottage," cried John. "It's the little house
where Vrouw van der Grift lives with her cat!"

"Oh, dear!" panted Sarah as the two children
stopped. "I do hope they can save it! Poor, poor
Vrouw van der Grift!"

"If a spark gets into that thatched roof, there'll be
no saving it," called another girl about Sarah's size
who was near her. "There aren't many thatched roofs
left in town now."

"There'll be one less by tonight," said a woman.

Sarah stood near John, watching. Sparks were
streaming out of the chimney of the little house.
Evidently the little old lady had built too hot a fire.
Soot in the chimney had caught fire and was burning

fiercely. The sparks fell on the dry thatch of the roof. There was a breeze blowing, and it fanned the sparks into flames.

The men were forming a bucket line. The long line reached from the river to the house. Big leather buckets were filled with water and then swung from one man to the next. The buckets were handed up to men who stood on the roofs of the nearest houses. From there they threw the water onto the burning thatch.

The fire hissed fiercely as the water fell upon it. But new sparks kept falling on the roof and new fires kept lighting. There was not nearly enough water.

Men ran in and out of the door of the burning house. They carried out the chairs and tables, the dishes and the kettles. Everything that could be moved was quickly carried to safety in a nearby house. In the doorway of the neighbor's house sat poor Vrouw van der Grift. She was in tears. Her white cat crouched in her arms. On the table behind her were piled her precious blue Delft platters and bowls from Holland. Her featherbed lay in a mass on the floor at her feet. Her quilts were piled on a chair. Her spinning wheel stood near.

"Oh, dear!" cried Sarah to John. "I do hope the

men can save the house. If only they had a hose!"

"And a fire engine!" said John.

"Why haven't those things been invented yet?" wailed Sarah.

"It's no use crying about it," said John unhappily.

It was becoming plain that the flames were spreading. One end of the roof was already blazing. The fire had crept into the thatch. All hope of saving the house was fast going, but the fight must be kept up. For if the flames spread the whole town might burn.

The children could see Governor Stuyvesant as he stamped up and down. He was giving orders. His first one was, "No one shall go inside the burning house again. It is no longer safe." Then he pointed this way and that way with his cane as he spoke. "That fence must be pulled down before it catches fire. That shed must be dragged away. Go quickly and bring oxen to pull this shed to a safe distance. If it catches fire, the house next door will burn. There is no telling where the flames will stop with such a breeze!"

People rushed here and there to do what the Governor bade them. Two men came with a pair of heavy oxen to drag off the shed. There was hammering and sawing and shouting as the fence was ripped apart.

Suddenly, above all the noise, a cry could be heard. It was Vrouw van der Grift. She came running out of her neighbor's house.

"My linen! My linen!" she screamed.

The *kas* had been too big to move. None of the men had thought of saving the linen inside it.

"Poor Vrouw van der Grift!" cried the women as they tried to comfort her. There seemed to be nothing that anyone could do beyond that.

John was busy helping to carry off the fence. Sarah ran to him and told him quickly what had happened. John dropped his load with a bang. A determined look came into his eyes. He pulled Sarah by the arm after him.

"Come on around to the garden, back of the house," he whispered excitedly. "The wind's in the other direction. The roof is not burning yet on that other side. There are no people around there. No one will see us."

The children slipped like shadows into a neighboring yard and then climbed the fence into the garden of the burning house.

"Quick!" whispered John. "The cat's window! It's big enough for me to get through. The chest's just inside."

"Oh, do you think you ought to?" whispered Sarah in horror.

All John answered was, "Boost!"

He gripped the window sill and gave a quick jump. Then he pulled himself up to the ledge. Sarah "boosted" from below. Just then men working on the roof of the next house saw the two children.

"Stop those children! Get away from there! It's dangerous to enter the house! It's forbidden."

"Oh, hurry, hurry!" cried Sarah as she jumped up and down under the window in excitement.

In another second John was inside the window. The door into the little hall had been left closed. That was very lucky for John. The hall was hot and smoky, but the flames had not yet reached it. He jerked open the doors of the *kas*.

The next minute a shower of linen came out of the window. Sheets, tablecloths, napkins whirling through the air — out they all came. Sarah was covered as though by a fall of snow. The next minute two men reached Sarah's side. They started to snatch her away from the burning house, but in an instant they, too, looked like snowmen come to life. More and more linen came flying out the window. The men saw what was happening. They began to laugh, and then they snatched up armfuls of linen and raced away with it to a safe place. Back they came for more and more. Sarah was half laughing and half crying as she too filled her arms.

Out came another piece of linen, six yards long. Then came a flurry of napkins — all of Vrouw van der Grift's one hundred napkins! Out the linens kept coming, until at last the *kas* was empty. John's eyes smarted with the smoke. He quickly climbed to the top of the chest. Then he slipped through the window and dropped to the ground. It was good to feel the fresh air again.

Now little Vrouw van der Grift came running through the garden, and stood there crying tears of happiness with her linen piled about her. The linen was wet and dirty, but what of that? Linen can be washed and bleached. It was saved. That was the important thing.

Vrouw van der Grift wanted to hug John, but the smoke had blackened his face. He was coughing and panting. One man emptied a bucket of water over his head. It felt cool and delicious. Another man gave him a cold drink. He began to feel better.

John stood with the water dripping from his nose,

rubbing smoke from his eyes. Suddenly he saw that someone was standing near him looking at him sternly. It was Governor Stuyvesant.

"You were forbidden to go into that house," said the Governor sternly. "I had given orders that no one else should go in. It was dangerous."

"Yes — yes, Your Excellency," stammered John. "But I knew just where the chest was, and about the cat's window. Nobody but a boy could get in that way, and — and — "

"Cat's window or no cat's window," growled the Governor, "orders are orders, young man!"

John looked up at him through his wet hair. A trickle of water was running down his nose. The Governor was scowling, but there seemed to be a twinkle in his eyes. John's courage rose.

"Yes, Your Excellency," he said, "but you know how the women are about their linen — "

"Women do not rule this town," said the Governor firmly, "nor children — yet!"

Stuyvesant turned on his wooden leg and went stomping away. Sarah and John watched him go. The tall slim figure was covered with a dark cape. In spite of the wooden leg, the Governor moved with grace and dignity.

"You know, I really like him," whispered John to Sarah.

By the middle of the afternoon there was nothing left of Vrouw van der Grift's house but charred brick walls and empty windows. At last the men stopped their work. Mopping their faces, they sat down wherever they could. The women brought them mugs of beer to drink. There was no danger now that the flames would spread, but a watch must be set. Two men at a time were ordered to stay by the ruins of the house, lest the night wind fan the ashes into fresh flames.

At last, one by one, the families started back to their homes Vrouw Hendricks gathered her brood about her. "Home," she called, "home again! It's past suppertime, and the dinner table not yet cleared!"

On the way home there was much talk of fires. "The Governor is right when he says we must have no more thatched roofs," said one neighbor to Vrouw Hendricks. "New Amsterdam is too large a city now for that sort of thing. It was all right when we were just a little town."

"Yes," said another woman, "and he is right when he warns us not to drop burning coals from the shovel when we carry them across the barnyard."

"Why does anyone want to carry burning coals around in a shovel?" cried Sarah in surprise. It sounded like a very queer thing to do.

"Well, well!" laughed the first woman. "It's clear to see that Vrouw Hendricks is a good housekeeper, or the child would never ask such a question."

Vrouw Hendricks smiled proudly. "When the fire is out in the morning," she explained to Sarah, "some people run to their neighbors for a shovelful of hot coals to start it with. It's easier than to get a spark with flint and steel. But I, I have had good luck. Each night I cover the red coals carefully. Each morning there are some left to start my fire. It must be five years since I lost the fire on my hearth!"

Just then the Hendricks family reached their home. They bade their neighbors good day and went in the door. Vrouw Hendricks looked about her kitchen. Then she gave a cry.

"My fire! My fire! Did I speak too soon?" she gasped. "We ran from the house so quickly that I did not bank it with ashes."

She hurried to the fireplace and knelt beside it. She poked carefully among the cold gray ash with her poker. At first there was no sign of life. Then one red eye glared from the gray ash. Vrouw Hendricks cried out joyfully. She snatched up a turkey wing and began to fan the one red coal. She fed it bits of dry straw and slivers of dry wood. Soon a tiny blaze flared up. Vrouw Hendricks sat back on her heels and beamed.

"Five years," she said, "and it still burns!"

Sarah looked at John. Then she leaned over and whispered. "Wouldn't she be surprised if she knew about matches?" But Sarah said it in a very soft whisper. She did not want to be put to bed with a bowl of herb tea!

Sarah had been thinking as she watched Vrouw Hendricks fanning the coals. Now she beckoned to John, and he followed her into the garden. "John," she said, "I have an idea. Couldn't you make some matches?"

"I don't know how," John said gravely. "Isn't it strange? Do you know, Sarah," he went on, "there are so many things we have in New York that it *seems* as though we ought to be able to tell these people how to make some of them. I've been thinking and thinking, but I haven't thought of anything yet. I can tell them about automobiles, but I can't *make* one. I can tell them about electric lights, but I can't even make a battery — not with what I can get hold of here. Isn't it queer?"

"I could tell them how to make school a great deal better," said Sarah firmly, "but no one would listen to me."

"They certainly wouldn't," said John with a sigh. "But thank goodness no one remembered school this afternoon!" Then he added, "I wish that schoolhouse would burn down!"

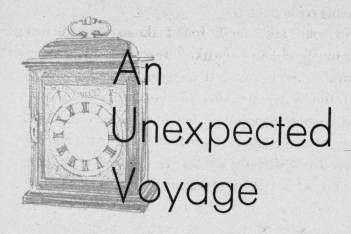

An Unexpected Voyage

JOHN CAME TO BREAKFAST next morning with the firm look in his eye that Sarah was getting to know so well.

"We're going to hunt for the tunnel today," he said softly to Sarah. "I'm not going back to that school!"

But Vrouw Hendricks had other plans for them. "Sarah and John," she said. "I want you to come to market with me. There is time before school. Get two big baskets."

So John and Sarah found themselves following Vrouw Hendricks to market. The market was on the Strand near the shore. It was a bright, beautiful day, and the water sparkled in the early-morning sun. The country people had left home before daybreak. Here were gathered a good company of them with many fresh things for sale. The children wandered about and watched with interest all that went on.

"Look!" exclaimed John as he saw an old man buying a measure of corn, "he's using wampum beads for money!"

Vrouw Hendricks, too, had her wampum with her. She bought a round Dutch cheese for fifteen beads and put it into Sarah's basket. Then she chose a tender young suckling pig for dinner, and then a basket of early peaches. Sarah and John soon found their baskets growing heavy.

At the far end of the market some Indians were selling turkeys and venison and maple sugar. One little Indian girl, no larger than Sarah, had a pile of baskets before her on the ground. Sarah smiled, and the Indian child smiled back. But there was no more time to linger, for Vrouw Hendricks was calling, "Come now, children, I must go to the Company's store for spice and sugar. Keep right with me. I don't want to lose you in all this crowd."

"Crowd indeed," thought Sarah, "she ought to see the subway!"

Vrouw Hendricks turned in at a large building beyond the fort. There was a wharf nearby. It was in this building that the Dutch West India Company stored the furs that were to be sent to Holland to be sold. It was here that they sold to the people those things that could not be raised or made on Manhattan Island.

It was cool inside the big room, and the light was dim. There were already many people inside. Sarah and John looked curiously about them. Some people were buying so much that they paid in beaver skins instead of wampum.

"That's odd!" said John. "Beaver skins are pretty queer money!"

The storekeeper was measuring out the precious spices that came from India and the Spice Isles. He measured them as carefully as though they were gold. The smell of cinnamon and nutmeg, cloves and all-spice, hung in the air. He gave Sarah and John bits of cinnamon bark to chew.

A neighbor joined Vrouw Hendricks. She seemed upset and worried. The two women began to chat.

"What do you think of the news? Yesterday the fire, and now this!" said the neighbor in a troubled voice.

"I could scarcely sleep, I was so worried. It's dreadful — simply dreadful. The English — "

Vrouw Hendricks glanced quickly toward Sarah and John. They heard her murmur, "The children, you know. We've not talked of it before them. We mustn't worry them." Then she said aloud, "John and Sarah, put down your baskets. Wait for me outside on the wharf. You can watch them loading the boat. There's one nearly ready to sail. I'll call when I need you."

Out into the bright sunlight went the children.

"What do you suppose they were talking about?" Sarah wondered.

"These Dutch people don't seem to like the English," said John. "I heard the boys talking about it last night. But I guess they won't trouble us. Come on down to the wharf."

Sarah followed him. "Where are these English?" she asked him.

"Oh, up in Plymouth and Boston," answered John. "You remember about the Pilgrims coming over on the *Mayflower*, don't you? Well, more and more English are coming to America; they seem to want the whole place. It's greedy of them, I say."

But their attention soon turned to other matters. The good ship *Dolphin* lay at anchor not far from the wharf. Small boats were carrying loads of furs and casks of food and water out to her. An old man stood nearby. "When does the boat sail?" John asked him.

"She's about loaded now," said the man. "When the tide's right and the wind's right, the captain will give the word and the sailors will hoist the sails. It may be today, or it may be tomorrow. It's all a matter of wind and tide. It's no easy thing to take so big a ship out of this harbor."

"Why, it's really no bigger than a ferryboat," John said softly to Sarah as he looked at the gaily painted boat. Sarah put up a warning finger to silence him, and John turned back to the old man.

"I'd like to go aboard that ship," he said.

"Would you, now?" said the old man with a pleasant smile. "I'm waiting to go myself. My son's the captain. I'm old Captain Peeks. He's young Captain Peeks. I sailed the seas for forty years, but now I stay at home by my own fire. What with pirates and smugglers and the English, the sea's no place for an old man. I've fresh eggs and a cheese here for my son. His mother sent them. She worries about him. Here comes the boat for me. Come, I'll take you along with me."

A small boat bumped its nose against the wharf.

"Oh, we mustn't go," cried Sarah. "It must be nearly time for school."

The firm look appeared on John's face again. "I'm not going to that school," he said. "You can go back if you want to."

For a dreadful minute Sarah hesitated. Should she go, or shouldn't she? Old Captain Peeks had climbed down into the boat. He was holding up his hand to help her. Before she knew it, Sarah had stepped down.

"Oh, John, do you think — " began Sarah again.

But John only repeated, "You can go back if you want to!" That was easier said than done, for the little boat was already well out from shore. Sarah gave a sigh and settled down to enjoy the trip.

The children and the old man climbed to the deck of the *Dolphin* by a rope ladder. Then Captain Peeks took John and Sarah all around the boat. He showed them the deck and the cabins and the front part of the ship, which he called the forecastle. The forecastle opened on the deck. John and Sarah, peering into it, saw a brick floor with a fire burning on it. This was where the cooking was done for all on board. A black kettle was already simmering over the low flame, and an old sailor sat beside it. Captain Peeks bent over the old man and shouted in his ear, "We've got visitors, Uncle."

The old sailor looked up and smiled.

"He's deaf — deaf as a doorpost," said old Captain Peeks. "He must be near a hundred. Makes me feel like a young man. He says he won't die on shore. It's not safe, he says. He must be aboard a ship and feel the sea under his feet. So we let him stay on the ship. He'll tell you stories of the old days."

"What's that you say?" asked the old sailor.

"I said that you'd tell them stories of the old days," shouted Captain Peeks, and the old sailor nodded.

It was cool in the shade of the forecastle, and John and Sarah sat down near the old man. Captain Peeks went off to find his son. The old sailor began to talk. He spoke softly at first. Then slowly his voice rose louder and stronger. For some reason John and Sarah did not seem able to take their eyes away from him.

"Stories of the old days," the old sailor was saying. "I should say I could. Ever heard of Henry Hudson?"

The children nodded their heads. "The Hudson River is named for him," said John softly, "and so is Hudson Bay?"

"Well," went on the old man, "you'd not think it, but I sailed with Henry Hudson on the *Half Moon* when I was just a lad. A pretty ship she was! We came sailing into this very harbor before there was any town here at all. First white men to come this way, we were. 'Twas the prettiest place you ever saw — trees and flowers all over, and the sweet smell of grapevines in the air. No houses or forts cluttering up the place in those days. Just woods and deer and Indians. You two young ones would have liked it, I can tell you!"

The old man looked at the children and smiled. But he did not really seem to see them. He seemed to be seeing other days and other times. He went on with his story: "No sooner had we come to anchor, out there yonder in the Great River, than along came the Indians. You should have seen them! They had big, long canoes, each made out of the trunk of a tree. Each canoe held twenty red men all paddling together, their naked bodies shining in the sun. When they came alongside the boat, they held up corn and tobacco and grapes. Fresh food looked good to us, after eating naught but hard biscuit and salt pork! We traded food for strips of cloth and bits of pewter. But we watched those savages pretty carefully. You never can tell with a strange people!"

The old man stopped for a minute; someone was

shouting on deck, but he could not make out what was happening. He went on with his own story: "Those Indian chiefs were grand-looking men, I will say, with feathers in their long black hair, and feathered cloaks on their shoulders, and fine furs about them. They were grand, tall men to look at. I wish you could have seen them! They could have gone before the King of England without shame."

The old man turned to his cooking, and for a few minutes stirred the kettle that hung over the fire. Then he went on with his tale: "I never expected to see the day when there'd be a fine big city like New Amsterdam on Manhattan Island — not I! Neither did Henry Hudson, for all he was such a canny one. But he hadn't come sailing way across the Atlantic Ocean looking for Indians, oh no! It's so long back now — more than fifty years — that people have forgot what he was looking for."

The old sailor fixed his bright old eyes on the two children. Sarah huddled closer to John, but John took a long breath. "I know!" he bellowed at the old man. "Hudson was looking for a way to sail to China, just the way Columbus was."

"Right you are, son," said the old sailor, and he gave a hoarse chuckle. "Hudson wanted to sail right through this here land and get to China. So up that river out there we went asailing, trying to get to China. It was exciting, I tell you, not knowing where we were agoing! Every time we rounded a bend, we'd all rush to look and see what was ahead.

"Sometimes the water grew wide, and then we'd say, 'Here we are, come to the Pacific Ocean!' Then the shores would close in narrow again. How the men did grumble! — and then grow quiet and sullen. You see, some of the men were against Hudson. They'd mutter that he was no good, and that they ought to kill him or throw him overboard and choose their own captain. But no one did anything — not then!

"Each day we would taste the water. You see, if it stayed salt, then we knew we were still on the sea. If it grew fresh, then we were just on a river, with no hope of ever sailing to China that way. Well, it was no good! All our hopes and all our threats couldn't make that water anything but a river. We sailed up that river for twenty days, and then we quit. It was no good. We went back home."

"It was the Hudson River, you know," John whispered to Sarah. "Of course Hudson couldn't get to China that way." Sarah nodded.

For a few minutes the old man sat silent, shaking

his head back and forth. Then suddenly he leaned toward the children. He raised one long thin finger. *"I'll never forget the face of Henry Hudson the last time I saw him,"* he said. *"I'll never forget that face. I may live to be a hundred, but I'll never forget!"*

The children sat awed and still as they watched the old man. Sarah gripped John's arm nervously. There was more shouting on deck. There were sounds of feet running back and forth, but the children paid no attention, for the old man was talking again.

"I can shut my eyes and see it as plain as day, this very minute," said the old man. "Sometimes I wake up at night dreaming I'm up there again."

Queer little chills began to run up and down Sarah's back. She moved closer to John. The old man went on with his tale: "Henry Hudson was pretty well broken up by that first trip, but he didn't give up — not he! He got another boat and started off again. I shipped with him for the second trip. This time he sailed north. He tried to get around this country to the north. Well, do you know what happened? We got up in the frozen north sea with icebergs floating around like shining glass mountains. The seabirds swooped around us, screaming and crying drearily. Seemed as though they knew what was going to happen. Then at last, the men wouldn't stand for no more. They wouldn't go on!"

The old man bent toward the children and whispered one word. "*Mutiny!* Do you know what that means?"

John and Sarah nodded.

"Mutiny," said the old man, "is when the sailors turn against their captain. They capture the guns and arms, and take over the ship. 'Twas a rough set of men Hudson had on the boat that last trip. When Hudson ordered them to sail that ship further into that frozen sea, they mutinied!"

There were calls and shouts from the deck. For a minute Sarah and John thought that a ragged crew of mutinous sailors would come bursting into the forecastle with drawn swords and fierce looks. But the noise died down, and the old man went on: "The sailors turned against Hudson, I say, and they put him and his young son, and seven of the sailors who were sick, in a small boat. There they left them, all alone floating in that strange cold, lonely sea. There were some of us who didn't want to do it. Yes, there were! But the others had the guns and the powder. If we'd disputed, we'd been left behind too."

The old man's voice trailed off into a hoarse whisper. He seemed to be seeing it all over again. "Off we sailed," he said slowly, "and I'll never forget the look on Hudson's face. He had his son beside him. The boy wasn't much older than you are. The boy was sitting up straight the last I saw of him, but Hudson was bent and broken. I'll never forget the look on his face — "

"What do you suppose happened to them?" whispered Sarah.

But the old sailor had stopped talking. He was living in other days and seeing other sights. The children sat silent and breathless. The old man seemed to hold them in a spell.

Suddenly John realized that, outside on deck, it had grown strangely quiet. There was only the creak of boards and the sound of the wind. A fresh breeze blew into the forecastle. Then he noticed that the floor was moving gently beneath his feet. It was rising and falling, rising and falling.

"What's happening?" cried John. He jumped to his feet and, pulling Sarah after him, ran out on deck. The shore was moving rapidly past them. While they had been listening to the old sailor, the boat had sailed.

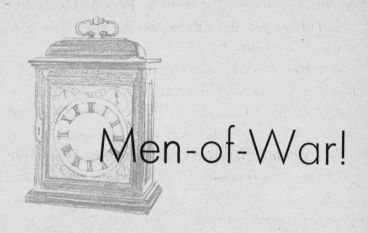

Men-of-War!

I<small>N HORROR</small>, John and Sarah stood on deck wondering what to do next. Then suddenly a sailor saw them and gave a cry that brought half a dozen men about the two children. The captain, too, came quickly to see what was the matter.

"What's this? What's this?" he demanded in no pleasant tone as he looked at the children. "Are these stowaways?"

Sarah began to cry — she just couldn't help it. She wanted to be brave and stand by John, and make him proud of her, but this was too much. "We didn't mean to come," she sobbed.

But John did not make fun of her tears. He put his hand on her arm and said softly, "I'll look out for you, Sarah." Then he turned to the captain. "We came aboard with your father, sir. He must have gone off and forgotten us. The old sailor was telling us a story."

The captain frowned. "A pretty pickle the old man has left for me! Whatever am I going to do with you?"

"Can't you take us back?" cried Sarah.

"No, I cannot!" said the captain firmly. "I'm well out toward the sea, and that is the direction I'm going to keep moving. There are strange things going on in these parts that you two don't understand. I'm making straight for Holland as fast as wind and sail can take me, and it will be six weeks or two months before we get there."

"Two months!" repeated Sarah in dismay.

"Yes," went on the captain, "and it may be all winter before a boat comes back — if one ever does," he added darkly. "It's these English that are making all the trouble. Some English boats are out there at sea right now, waiting for us, and they have no good intentions! 'Twill be only by the grace of God that we can slip by them. I've troubles and worries enough without having two children on my hands!" The captain turned away impatiently. He began to pace up and down the deck, calling an order here and there to a sailor.

But with all the difficulties John could not help feeling the thrill and excitement of going to sea. A fresh salt breeze was blowing. The ship was speeding along through the green water. Great white sails billowed above him, against the bright-blue sky, and sailor boys were calling to one another as they climbed out along the yards to let out more sail.

Before John thought what he was saying, he exclaimed, "My, I'd like to be able to climb like that!"

"You would?" asked the captain suspiciously as he stopped by the two children. "You're sure you didn't play this prank on purpose?"

"I'll not take a girl with me when I do that, sir," answered John. For the first time the captain gave John a friendly glance. That did not help to decide what should be done, but it made matters easier between them.

The mate stopped by the captain and touched his hat. "We might lower a small boat and send the children ashore on Long Island," he suggested. "There are English families there."

The captain shook his head. "I'll have nothing to do with the English," he said. "The further we keep from the English, the better!"

Again Sarah felt tears stinging her eyes, but this time she choked them back. She held tightly on to John's arm. Everything else she knew in the world seemed to be fast leaving her. She was not going to let *him* go. And now for the first time John too felt a lump rise in his throat as he looked back for a last glimpse and saw how fast New Amsterdam was disappearing behind them. The boat was now passing the Narrows and was rapidly making for the open sea.

"Well," said John, just for something to say, "Sarah, if we do have to go to Holland for the winter, we'll see canals and windmills and everything."

It was too much for Sarah. "What will my mother say?" she sobbed. "What will both our mothers say?"

The captain had been walking impatiently up and down the deck. As Sarah spoke he turned toward her, and seeing her tears said, in an almost kind voice, "Well, we'll work out something, child. Don't cry! You two go down to the forecastle and get something to eat. You must be hungry."

In the forecastle they found their friend, the old sailor. He gave them each a bowl of bean soup. At home, neither Sarah nor John would have touched bean soup. But the forecastle of a sailing ship and an apartment in New York were two very different places. Sarah and John ate their soup in silence and thankfully.

When they had finished, the old sailor sat down beside them and asked, "What are your names?"

"Sarah and John," shouted John.

"Speak a little louder, son," said the old man. "A little louder."

John took a long breath and put his mouth to the old man's ear. "John and Sarah," he shouted.

"John and Sarah," repeated the old man. "You don't say so! Why those were the names of the first white babies to be born in these parts. John Vinje was born before there was scarcely a house built. Sarah Rappelye came along soon after. She was born up the river, but they brought her down to the town while she was still a toddler. Cute thing she was, too! Smart as they make 'em. *John and Sarah* — those are good names in these parts."

Sarah looked at John in surprise. "Do you suppose," she said, "that our names have anything to do with all these strange things that are happening to us?"

"I don't know," said John. "I can't understand what's happening any more, anyway!"

The old man went back to his cooking. The children could hear him chuckling to himself. "John and Sarah," he kept saying. "Well I remember those two little kippers. Bright as buttons they were. They thought nothing of being born in the wilderness — not they!"

John and Sarah sat and watched the old man, and wondered what was going to happen to them next. Suddenly there was a loud cry outside. The old man did not hear it, but John and Sarah ran out on deck. Then they heard it again.

"Sail to starboard! Sail to starboard!"

The voice seemed to come from the sky. The children put back their heads and shaded their eyes. Far up the main mast stood the watchman in the crow's-nest.

Several sailors came running to the rail to look. Sarah and John joined them. Way off on the horizon was a tiny speck. Slowly it grew larger.

"Why," said John, "it's no bigger than one of those toy boats in the pond in Central Park!"

Captain Peeks was standing near them. "It will be

bigger than we want it to be before we're through," he muttered.

John looked up at him hopefully. "Do you think it might be a pirate ship, sir?" he asked.

"It's worse than a pirate ship, I'm thinking," said the captain, and that was all he would say.

"You don't think it might be willing to take us back to New Amsterdam," suggested Sarah.

"I do not!" said the captain. Then he left to give orders to the men.

Suddenly there was another cry from the man in the crow's-nest. "*A second sail to starboard! A second sail to starboard!*"

There was more excited talk among the sailors as they hurried about the boat. John and Sarah, standing alone at the rail, watched the two sails grow larger and larger.

"What do you think it all means?" Sarah wondered, but John could not answer.

In this new excitement they forgot their troubles for the moment. It was rather fun standing at the rail. Even Sarah enjoyed it. The breeze tossed her hair about and made John's stand up straighter than ever. It made their cheeks pink and their eyes bright, and every now and then it blew spray into their faces. If only they had been going toward home instead of away from it! Then the trip would really have been fun instead of a time of worry about what was to happen to them. There was worry now, too, as to what was to happen to everyone on the ship.

By noon there was another call from the crow's-nest. *"The vessels to starboard are men-of-war. They fly the English flag."*

"But why do the English send battleships against *us?*" cried Sarah in amazement.

The captain heard her. "They want to capture New Amsterdam and all the country round it," he said bitterly. "They're no better than thieves and pirates. The Dutch bought that land from the Indians. The Dutch cleared the trees off it, and they made their homes there. They've never done the English any harm. Now the English want to step in and take it away from them. They're thieves and rascals, every one of them!"

The captain turned away with an angry snort. Sarah looked at John, her eyes wide with astonishment.

"So that's why they have all been talking so much about the English!" she exclaimed. "The English want to capture New Amsterdam!"

"I'm beginning to understand a great many things,"

said John, and he looked darkly at the two oncoming boats.

As the long afternoon wore on, many things happened. Sarah and John watched breathlessly. At first Captain Peeks tried to run the *Dolphin* past the English vessels. He turned her bow sharply to the south, and hoisted all the sail that she could carry. The boat seemed to fly over the waves, but the English men-of-war were too fast for her. Swiftly and surely they bore down upon the Dutch boat. They drew so near that Sarah and John could see the men on deck. They could see the cannon and the gunners beside them.

At midafternoon there was a sudden flash of fire, a deep *bo-o-om bang*. A great splash of water spilled over the deck of the *Dolphin*. The English had fired a shot across the bow of the Dutch ship! What would they do now? Would they send the next ball through her hull and sink her? The captain called out orders sharply and sailors clambered like monkeys up the rigging. The boat seemed alive with men.

When John and Sarah saw the captain again he said, "Bad news for us and bad news for New Amsterdam, but it may be good news for you two. I'm turning the ship back to port. We can't make it. There's nothing to do but go back to New Amsterdam and throw in our luck with the town."

"But what do you suppose they'll do to the town?" cried John, aghast. "Will they shoot cannon balls into it?"

"They can wreck every house on Manhattan Island with those guns," growled the captain, and then he hastened away. Even as he spoke, the children could feel the boat shifting her course. In a few minutes the helmsman had swung her around. She started bravely tacking back against the wind. And back she went toward New Amsterdam.

A great weight seemed to be lifted from John's heart. At least they were going back to land. As for Sarah, she suddenly wanted to shout and sing. To herself she chanted, "Back, back, back to New Amsterdam. Back, back, back to New Amsterdam!"

It was late that night when the *Dolphin* sailed safely through the Narrows and into the bay. Near Staten Island the captain ordered the anchor dropped. All sails were furled, and the masts rose bare and stark against the night sky. Tired sailor boys, who had done double work that day, dropped wearily down to sleep wherever they were. A watch was set. Then a great quiet settled over the vessel, like a blanket of stillness. The stars shone bright in the sky, and the little waves of the harbor lapped gently against the sides of the boat.

Sarah yawned, and even John could scarcely keep his eyes open. They found their way to the cabin they were to sleep in — one of the two small cabins that were all the boat could boast. The cabin was nearly filled with sea chests, rolls of blankets and quilts, and casks of food. John and Sarah kept stumbling over them in the dim light. A candle in a tin lantern hung from a peg in the wall. The cabin was hot and stuffy; and now that there was no sea breeze, strange smells and odors filled the ship.

"How would you like to live here for two months?" John asked.

"No, thank you," said Sarah, as she spread a quilt on the hard wooden bunk.

"Well, I suppose the *Mayflower* was something like this boat, and the Pilgrims stood it," John mused. He went to the door and looked out. "Look, Sarah," he said, "see that light over there? It must be about where the fort is. I wonder what's happening in New Amsterdam tonight."

Sarah was too tired to look. She climbed into one end of the bunk and shut her eyes. John blew out the candle and then slipped into the other end. It was a hard bed, but neither one had time to notice. In a moment, they were both fast asleep.

Little did they know that the light they had seen

was a bonfire giving light to men who worked all night on the fort. That very day the English had sent men to demand that Governor Stuyvesant surrender the town to them. They said that if he would give up without fighting, they would do no harm to the town. But if he fought them, they would turn their guns upon New Amsterdam.

Governor Stuyvesant Decides

FOR SEVERAL DAYS the *Dolphin* lay in hiding off Staten Island. John and Sarah sat in the sun on deck and wondered what was going to happen. The waiting seemed very long and very dull to them. Now and again bits of news reached the ship. Once a fishing boat came alongside, and there was hurried and excited talk. Once the captain sent men ashore to find out what they could from the nearest farm.

The news of what had happened was shouted to the old deaf sailor. He went about his work muttering, "I've seen the first house built on Manhattan Island. I don't want to live to see the last one blown to bits by English guns!"

At last John got up courage to ask a question that had been on his mind. He stopped beside the captain and said, "Do you think, sir, that the Dutch *might* give up the city without fighting? Do you think Governor Stuyvesant *might* surrender?"

The captain gave the boy an odd look. "My son," he said, "as I make it out from the news that reaches us, that's what the people want him to do. But think of it, lad, think of asking a man like Governor Stuyvesant to give up without fighting! He loves that town as he loves his own sons. 'Twould tear the very heart out of him!"

"It would," agreed John soberly, as he thought of the tall brave figure of the Governor. "He's no coward."

That night the captain decided that he could wait no longer. He would cross to New Amsterdam in a small boat. At least he would try to. "I'll take the children home to their parents and get rid of them," he said to his mate. "There are guards watching, but I think we can slip through. I know this harbor better than my own front yard."

It was a joy to have something happen at last, after all the uncertain waiting. Sarah began to dance about on the deck of the ship. John could scarcely wait to climb down the rope ladder into the little boat below. There were four stout sailors to row them, and a mast and sail in case they dared raise them. At last all was ready. Sarah waved good-by to the crew and to the old deaf sailor and to the *Dolphin*. Then the little boat slipped off into the darkness of the night.

"I'm glad to be going home at last," Sarah sighed happily.

"It's a long pull across the bay, and you're not home yet," the captain said grimly. "You may end this night in the hold of an English ship or in the bottom of the bay!"

The captain whispered an order to the sailors to keep close to land. The men pulled quietly but steadily at their oars. The little boat rose and fell gently on the waves. The air was cool and fresh against their faces. Soon Sarah fell asleep, but John sat up straight, watching everything. It was after midnight before he could make out the long low line of Manhattan Island. Then he saw the dark fort and the windmill beside it, against the night sky. Dark hulks were lying in the water near the fort — the two English men-of-war. John gasped when he saw how near the town they were. What if the cannon on their deck should suddenly be fired!

The first streak of light was in the east when the small boat grated on the beach. A guard, watching, came quickly toward them. "Who goes there?"

"It's I, Captain Peeks of the *Dolphin,*" came the low answer. "The English turned my boat back with a cannon ball. She's in hiding off Staten Island. I want to come ashore."

"Very well," was the answer, "but New Amsterdam is a sad place to come to."

The sailors jumped out into the shallow water and dragged the boat in as far as they could. One of them carried Sarah ashore, but John waded in with the men. Through the dark streets of the little town they went, behind the guard with his lantern.

The town seemed to be quiet and sleeping, but the first knock brought Mynheer Hendricks to the door. Vrouw Hendricks was just behind him, peering anxiously over his shoulder. They were fully dressed. Houses might be dark, but few people except the very old and the very young were sleeping in these troubled times.

When the Hendricks saw the children, there were cries of joy, and Sarah flew into Vrouw Hendricks' arms. There were hugging and kissing, laughter and tears. There were questions and questions, then answers and more questions.

In another minute brothers and sisters came tumbling out of their cupboard beds to greet the wanderers. The twins woke up and cried for Sarah. Vrouw Hendricks threw a handful of shavings on the fire, and it blazed up. The flames lighted up the shining pewter and brass, and their shadows danced on the walls of the snug room.

At last Vrouw Hendricks sat down and wiped her eyes. "Well," she said, "I'm glad you're back, but this is a sad time for New Amsterdam. You might be safer on the sea!"

"Well, whatever happens, I'm glad I'm here," said Sarah firmly. "I like it better on land."

"What do you think will happen, sir?" asked John of Mynheer Hendricks. "Do you think Governor Stuyvesant will fight?"

"It's hard to say," said Mynheer Hendricks. "The English promise they'll do us no harm if we surrender. They have two battleships, with their guns pointing right at us."

"Yes, I saw them," put in John.

"The English have no business here," went on Mynheer Hendricks bitterly, "but what can we do? We've few guns and less powder. Governor Stuyvesant is as brave as anyone could be, but what can he do? Sometimes it's braver to give in than to fight. Well, tomorrow we will know."

"It's the Duke of York who has sent over those boats," cried Vrouw Hendricks. "He's brother to the King of England, and a bad one, so I hear. What right has he to come stealing our homes or blowing them to bits about our ears? Did he ever do a hard day's work in his life?"

"There, there," said Mynheer Hendricks, "we must try to be calm and quiet, whatever the good Lord brings to us."

Suddenly there was a rattling outside, then a knock on the door. "Too much noise and too many lights," came the warning voice of the night watchman. "Quiet and dark in every house."

"Oh dear, dear, I'd forgotten!" cried Vrouw Hendricks. She quickly helped the children into their beds and banked the fire. Soon all was dark and quiet again.

With morning came the great question on everyone's lips and in everyone's heart: "*What will Gover-*

nor Stuyvesant do?" Little work was done in any house that day. Dishes were left upon the table. Floors were left unswept. Everyone, big and little, flocked to the Town Hall to wait for news. People wandered up and down. Everyone seemed frightened and helpless.

There was much coming and going during the morning. Messengers came from the English ships. They were gay to look upon in their red coats, trimmed with gold braid. Sarah and John watched them with wonder.

"How could anyone fight with those uniforms on?" said John.

"I'm sure I don't know," answered Sarah.

"I pray from the bottom of my heart there'll be no fighting of any sort!" said Vrouw Hendricks as she held the twins by the hand.

Now and again angry voices floated out from the windows of the Town Hall. There seemed to be much talk and argument going on. At times Governor Stuyvesant's voice could be heard shouting above the others.

"Oh, he must surrender. He must!" whispered Sarah to John.

"He'll make up his mind for himself," answered John. "He's not one to be afraid."

"There's little he can do, poor man," sighed Vrouw Hendricks.

Sarah and John glanced toward the battleships. They were anchored so close to shore that they could see the gunners and the guns. What could Governor Stuyvesant do against them?

At last came word. People pushed forward to hear it. *"The Governor is making terms with the English. He will give up the fort. The town is saved! The town is saved!"*

Shouts and cheers rose in the air. People laughed and cried, and ran about shaking hands. Boys threw their hats in the air and danced Indian war dances.

Mynheer Hendricks came out of the Town Hall and joined his family. He seemed sad and old, but he smiled at Vrouw Hendricks as he picked up one of the twins and hugged her.

Then he turned to John. "So you got back just in time to see the last of New Amsterdam, son," he said gravely. "Even the name of the town is to be changed, I hear. We're to be called *New York* from now on, named for the rascal who sent those ships over to capture us."

Sarah looked at John. *"So that's how it came to be New York,"* she gasped.

"Hush, watch out!" warned John.

At that moment the great doors of the Town Hall were flung open. Everyone turned to watch. Out of the door stalked His Excellency, Governor Stuyvesant, with his head held high. Down the steps he stomped, with his cane and his wooden leg. A silence fell over the crowd as he came nearer. People dropped back. Quietly they opened a path for him to pass through. He looked neither to right nor to left. He spoke to no one.

Through the crowd went Governor Stuyvesant, and down the lane that led to his home. Suddenly John pulled Sarah's arm. "Come on!" he whispered. "I want to speak to him, I want to tell him something."

"Do you think you'd better?" asked Sarah, but John pulled her after him. The two ran after Stuyvesant, and at his front door they overtook him.

"Your Excellency!" panted John.

The dark figure turned slowly round, and the Governor looked sternly at the boy. John remembered to snatch off his hat. Sarah bobbed a curtsy.

"What do you want with me?" asked the Governor.

"I — I just wanted to say, Your Excellency," the boy stammered. "I just wanted to tell you that we're sorry, terribly sorry, and — and — "

"Yes, we are — " put in Sarah.

It was hard for John to find the right words, but he went on bravely. "And I wanted you to know that New York won't forget you, sir. Nobody will care anything about the Duke of York, but everybody will remember you, Your Excellency. Everybody in New York will know about Peter Stuyvesant."

John stopped, breathless. The Governor laid his hand on the boy's head. He smiled a grim smile, but once again John felt that there was a light in his eye —

a light of understanding. Then the Governor turned and went into his own home. The door closed behind him.

Sarah and John stood looking at each other. Then very slowly, without a word, they started walking back toward their home.

All at once John stopped short. He pointed to a clump of bushes. "Sarah, will you look at that!" he cried. "I never saw that before!"

Sarah looked at the spot. There, almost hidden by the bushes, she saw something dark. They ran to see what it was.

"*It's the opening to a tunnel!*" cried John. He got down on his knees and peered in. Then carefully he started to crawl into it.

"Come on, Sarah," he called back. "Follow me!"

For a moment Sarah paused. She looked back at the little town behind her, now no longer Dutch but English. She would have liked to have a chance to say good-by to Vrouw Hendricks. Good mothers were good mothers at any time, she felt — in New Amsterdam or in New York. But John was calling to her to come. So Sarah dropped to her knees and crawled after him.

As they went on, they found that the tunnel grew

higher and wider. Soon they were able to get to their feet. There was a dim light far ahead, and they walked carefully toward it.

"Why, it's an old tumbledown subway station," cried John.

They climbed onto the platform and went toward a change booth. An old man sat inside. He looked strangely like the old deaf sailor. He was muttering to himself, but the children could not hear what he said. John ran eagerly up to him.

"How much is the fare?" he asked politely.

"Six beads of wampum," muttered the old man, "and don't ask me to change any beaver skins. I'll change no more beaver skins today!"

John drew out of his pocket the little deerskin bag that Vrouw Hendricks had given him. Inside were the twelve beads of wampum he had earned by weeding carrots. He counted out the beads and gave them to the old man.

John and Sarah stood looking around, but everything seemed strange and confused in the dim light. Suddenly a train pulled silently into the station and stopped. The doors opened. John and Sarah stepped quickly inside one of the cars, and the door closed behind them.

"Look at
the Clock!"

John LOOKED UP, confused. *They were in the same subway train from which they had started out!* He walked over to the subway guard who was standing near the door.

"Excuse me," said John. "What's the next station, please?"

"Eighty-sixth Street, son," the guard told him.

"Thanks," said John. "Sarah, that's our stop!"

The train roared into the brightly lighted station and stopped with a jerk. John took Sarah's arm. "Come on," he said, and they stepped quickly onto the platform. For a moment the floor seemed to sway under Sarah's feet. Then she followed John out through the turnstile.

They walked slowly along the passage that led to the street. At the foot of the stairs John hesitated. Then he stopped.

"Sarah," he said slowly, "Do you realize it's as if we've been away *for three hundred years?* Do you suppose we'll find everything changed when we get up those stairs? Are we going into the future now?"

There was a look of horror on Sarah's face. "Then where will Mother be?" she wailed. "Where will the apartment be after three hundred years?"

Sarah felt like running to find the tunnel and the way back to Vrouw Hendricks. This was worse than being found by an Indian! Or being carried off on a boat! Or being fired at by the English!

She and John stood looking at each other, white-faced. Then John took a deep breath and called, "Come on, Sarah!" They ran upstairs to the street.

For a minute they stood looking about them. High buildings rose on all sides. Trucks and cars and buses hurried by. It was late afternoon, and the street was filled with people hurrying home. It was exactly the same city they had left behind!

"Look Sarah!" John almost whispered in joyous disbelief. "Look at the clock!"

"Why, it's almost the same time we left," said Sarah — "it's as if — as if — *time stood still while we were gone!*"

"There's my apartment house!" cried John.

"And our mothers probably just got back!" cried Sarah.

"Let's go home!" said John. "Come on."

The lights turned from green to red. John took Sarah's hand and hurried her across the street.